this plus that

LIFE'S LITTLE EQUATIONS

AMY + KROUSE + ROSENTHAL = WRITER

JEN + CORACE = ARTIST

HARPER

An Imprint of HarperCollinsPublishers

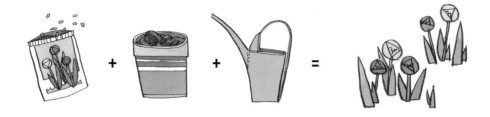

This Plus That: Life's Little Equations

Text copyright © 2011 by Amy Krouse Rosenthal

Illustrations copyright © 2011 by Jen Corace

Manufactured in China.

Library of Congress Cataloging-in-Publication Data
Rosenthal, Amy Krouse.
        This plus that : life's little equations / Amy + Krouse + Rosenthal = writer ;
Jen + Corace = artist. — 1st ed.
                p.   cm.
        Summary: Simple arithmetical equations show how big and small
moments add up in life.
        ISBN 978-0-06-172655-2 (trade bdg.)
        ISBN 978-0-06-172656-9 (lib. bdg.)
        [1. Arithmetic—Fiction.   2. Conduct of life—Fiction.]   I. Corace, Jen,
ill.   II. Title.   III. Title: This plus that.
PZ7.R719445Th   2010   2008034357
[E]—dc22   CIP
                                                         AC

Typography by Martha Rago
12 13 14 15 SCP 10 9 8 7 6 5 4 ❖ First Edition

Maria + Modugno = dedication

—A.K.R.

To Leonard H. Pants

—J.C.

1 + 1 = us

yes + no

= maybe

red + blue = purple   blue + yellow = green   yellow + red = orange

red + orange + yellow + green + blue + indigo + violet = rainbow

smile + wave = hello

big buildings + bustling = city

smile + ocean wave = beach

winding roads + rustling = country

chalk + sitting = school

chalk + jumping = hopscotch

laughter + keeping secrets + sharing = best friend

somersaults + somersaults + somersaults

= dizzy

wishes + frosting = birthday

anything + sprinkles = better

violin
    + flute
        + saxophone
           + cello
              + trumpet
                  + clarinet
                      + percussion

= symphony

blaming + eye rolling ≠ sincere apology

"I'm sorry" + hug = sincere apology

small + bottle = baby

tall + coffee = grown-up

dark + popcorn = movie

mumbling + toe staring ≠ polite

handshake + "how are you" = polite

leaves + hot soup = fall

(snow + carrot) + rosy cheeks = winter

birds + buds = spring

barefoot + screen door + popsicles = summer

balloon + wind = lost

practice + practice = learning

practice + practice + practice = mastering

chores ÷ everyone = family

soul + $\left\{\begin{array}{l}\text{color = art} \\ \text{words = literature} \\ \text{sound = music} \\ \text{movement = dance}\end{array}\right.$

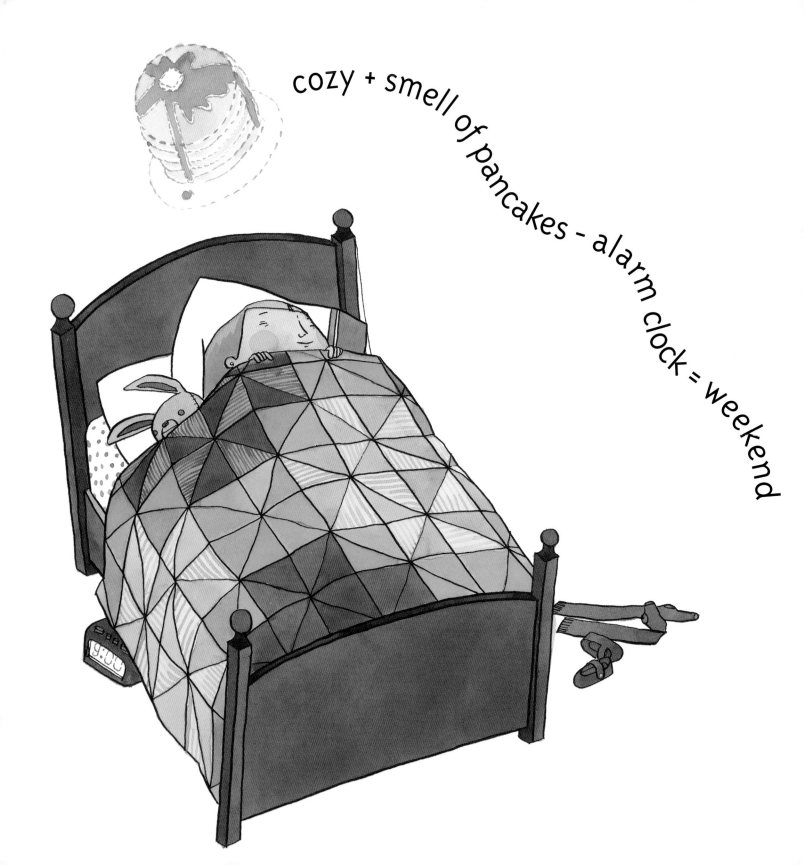

cozy + smell of pancakes - alarm clock = weekend

good days + bad days = real life

once upon a time + happily ever after = pretend

(every star in the sky + the sun + the moon) × my heart = love you to the infinite power

all done + time to go = the end